SUPER HAPPY PARTY BEARS

GNAWING AROUND

SUPER HAPPY PARTY BEARS

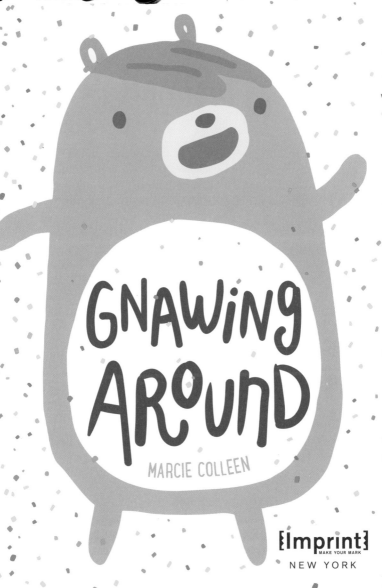

GNAWING AROUND

MARCIE COLLEEN

【Imprint】
MAKE YOUR MARK
NEW YORK

[Imprint] MAKE YOUR MARK

A part of Macmillan Children's Publishing Group

SUPER HAPPY PARTY BEARS: GNAWING AROUND. Copyright © 2016 by Imprint.
All rights reserved. Printed in China by Toppan Leefung Printing Ltd.,
Dongguan City, Guangdong Province. For information,
address Imprint, 175 Fifth Avenue, New York, N.Y. 10010.

Library of Congress Cataloging-in-Publication Data is available.
ISBN 978-1-250-09807-8 (paperback) / ISBN 978-1-250-10674-2 (ebook)
Our books may be purchased in bulk for promotional, educational,
or business use. Please contact your local bookseller or the Macmillan
Corporate and Premium Sales Department at (800) 221-7945 ext. 5442
or by e-mail at MacmillanSpecialMarkets@macmillan.com.

Book design by Natalie C. Sousa
Imprint logo designed by Amanda Spielman
Illustrations by Steve James

First Edition—2016

1 3 5 7 9 10 8 6 4 2

mackids.com

If this book isn't yours, keep your thieving paws off it. Obey or may the
elastic string on all of your party hats snap before you even get them on.

TO THE THREE E'S WITH LOVE

CHAPTER ONE

Welcome to the Grumpy Woods!

Just kidding. No one is welcome here. Turn around and go back. The Grumpy Woods doesn't need any new residents—and it especially doesn't need any more bears. Especially not bears who like to dance and sing and make doughnuts and have parties. If you are a bear, then *stay out.*

Of course, right now you might be thinking, *Bears are cute* and *Parties are fun.* Cut it out. The animals of the Grumpy Woods do not agree, because everyone here who's not a bear is, well, *grumpy*.

So don't bother looking for a

welcome sign, because it's been taken down. All welcome mats and mailboxes have also been removed. That's right. They were

all taken down by an official
decree of the mayor.

Mayor Quill had an official
meeting at City Hall. (City Hall is
really just an upturned log, not

actually a hall of any sort, but don't tell Mayor Quill that. He takes his position quite seriously.)

The Super Happy Party Bears were not invited to the meeting.

At that meeting, everyone— from Bernice Bunny to Humphrey Hedgehog—decided that *no one* was welcome in the Grumpy Woods

and that anything welcoming
should be removed.

They voted. And that was that.
It was very official.

And so, every day, everyone in
the Grumpy Woods wakes up on
the wrong side of the bed, puts on
their cranky pants (actually, more
like a whole outfit), and orders

up some breakfast—two scoops
of crabby in a bowlful of *Leave me
alone!* That is, everyone except the
Super Happy Party Bears.

Over at the Party Patch, the
Headquarters of Fun—where the
Super Happy Party Bears have made
their home—life is very different.

LIFE IS SUPER. Life

is happy. And life is full of parties!

Remember the mailboxes and
the welcome mats? They were
mentioned about seven paragraphs
ago. Well, you will find that
they have been relocated
to the Party Patch. The

mailboxes dangle like ornaments from the shrubbery. The welcome mats are stacked like a house of cards to create a cozy canopy in front of the main entrance. The main entrance is easy to find because carefully placed sticks, laid out in the shape of arrows, lead any would-be visitor up a flower-lined path, straight to the Super Happy Party Bears' den.

Oh, and that welcome sign? Well, that can be found at the Party Patch, too. On top of the sign sits a little stick-figure diorama that includes the likeness of a few Grumpy Woods neighbors.

10

They are wearing party hats and dancing. The leader of the party appears to be Mayor Quill.

See, while the others in the Grumpy Woods can't stand the bears, the Super Happy Party Bears *adore* their neighbors, especially Mayor Quill.

And so, on a beautiful morning such as this, the Super Happy Party Bears get up on the cheeriest side of the bed, put on their pants of positivity, and order up some breakfast—two triple-decker giggle-and-jelly sandwiches and a bowlful of *The best day ever!*

Nothing annoys the critters of the Grumpy Woods more.

Except when the bears have a
party.

And they are always having a

13

2

CHAPTER TWO

Mayor Quill was on some very important official business.

Angrily clutching a stack of envelopes in his paw, he stomped up the path marked with twig arrows and lined with cheerful flowers. Signs along the way pointed to the Party Patch. Sounds of celebration were coming out of the shrubs up ahead—it sounded like the song "If You're Happy and You Know It," complete with a pots-and-pans rhythm section. It sounded like a party—a *breakfast party.*

And then he was in front of it—
the welcome sign.

Mayor Quill squinted at the tiny
Mayor Quill stick figure dancing
atop the wooden sign, and his
quills bristled.

"That tiny party hat makes me look fat," he mumbled, and bumped into the sign on purpose as he waddled by, hoping to topple it. But to his dismay, the mayor stick figure simply tipped into the other stick neighbors in a kind of group hug.

"BAH!" griped Mayor Quill as he crumpled the letters in his paw.

For a week now, Mayor Quill had been getting these letters. He kept finding them all over

City Hall. With no mailbox for his mail, Mayor Quill was finding letters under his pillow, inside his morning bowl of leaves and berries, and even in his underwear drawer! And they all said the most annoying things:

Who's the best mayor around? You are!

You're Swell.

Way 2 Go!

The cheery letters had the paw prints of the Super Happy Party

Bears all over them, and Mayor Quill was fed up.

He started to cram the letters under the door. The breakfast bash abruptly stopped, and the mayor heard the shuffle of a dozen pairs of furry feet gather on the other side.

"ONE! TWO! THREE! WHO CAN IT BEEEEEEEEEE?" sang the bears, before swinging the door open wide.

19

"QUILLY!" they all cheered.

Mayor Quill threw up his hands
in surprise, and the envelopes flew
into the air.

"He's delivering *mail* to us," said
the littlest bear as he gathered up
the wrinkled envelopes.

And before Mayor Quill could
object, he was pulled into the

Party Patch and a cup of juice put
in his paw.

"I'm actually here on very
important official business
regarding this mail," said Mayor
Quill.

"This is the most special morning
ever!" cheered the bears. "It's
official! This calls for another party!

"IT'S SUPER HAPPY PARTY
TIME! SUPER HAPPY PARTY TIME!"
the bears chanted, and they did
their Super Happy Party Dance.

Slide to   the right.

Hop to   the left.

Shimmy, shimmy, shake.

Strike a pose.

"We must provide refreshments for this party!" announced a small bear, breaking his dance pose. It was Mops, named for his mop-top hair that fell over his eyes.

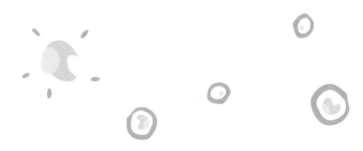

"This isn't a party," said Mayor Quill. "More like a meeting."

"A meeting is just a party without doughnuts," said Bubs as he calmly blew party-perfect bubbles. Bubs was always the voice of party wisdom.

"DOUGHNUTS!" they all cheered, and scrambled off in a flurry.

Pans clattered and batter
splattered everywhere as the

bears busied themselves preparing the doughnuts. Meanwhile, the littlest bear delivered the mail.

"'You're swell.' This one must be for you." He handed the letter to Shades, who winked over his star glasses. And to a bear who was doing jumping jacks he said, "'Way 2 Go!' is definitely meant for you, Jacks."

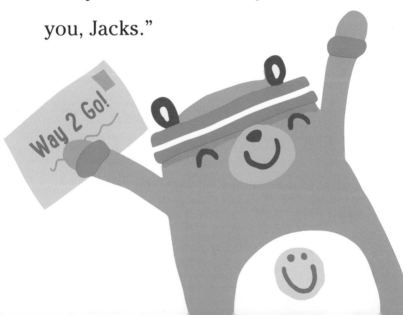

The littlest bear then hesitated. "'Who's the best mayor around?' Silly, Quilly! That's YOU!"

"These letters were—" the mayor protested.

"—meant to make us happy?" asked the bears sweetly. "THEY DID!"

Just then, Mayor Quill felt a tug on one of his back quills. He turned around to see a bear wearing some sort of armor made out of twigs and pinecones.

"What in the world are you wearing?" he asked.

"It's the newly patented Hug-a-Mayor suit. It allows us to hug a porcupine such as yourself repeatedly, and for longer periods, without getting poked."

The mayor backed away awkwardly from the outstretched padded arms. There was nothing Mayor Quill hated more than hugs. Except for maybe stumbling backward and sitting right in a big bowl of doughnut batter.

He didn't want hugs, or

doughnuts, or mail, or a party.

The mayor just wanted a bath.

CHAPTER THREE

Mayor Quill plucked a fresh sharp
quill from his backside and flicked
off a bit of batter before dipping the
quill into his inkpot. He carefully
added to the Mayoral Decree he
had hung on the tallest tree at the
center of the woods. It was basically

a list of rules to follow—but the

porcupine liked the sound of the

word *decree*. It was very official.

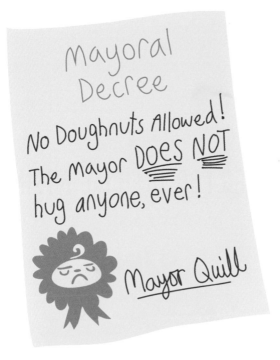

He underlined the words *DOES*

and *NOT*—not once, not twice,

but five times. He was not messing around.

He stepped back to examine his work and shook his rump a little, trying to shake off the goopy mess. It was time for a long, hot bath.

Mayor Quill hung his CLOSED FOR OFFICIAL BUSINESS sign on his door and then stepped inside the official City Hall—which was really just the log he lived in—and went to his private, members-only watering hole, of which he was the only member. He cued up the whirlpool for his bubble bath.

Of course, the whirlpool was really just Arlo Rabbit, kicker extraordinaire, who could strike up a current in the calmest of

waters with his hind legs and who
didn't mind the exercise. Arlo was
good about covering his eyes to
give Mayor Quill privacy.

But when the mayor stepped into the tub he had made by carving a knot out of the log, the water level seemed incredibly low.

"That's odd," he muttered. "You have your work cut out for you today, Arlo."

Just then there was a knock at the trunk.

Mayor Quill wanted nothing more than to soak in the tub, rid his tush of doughnut batter, and get on with his day. He ignored the knock.

Knock, knocky, knock-knock.

Mayor Quill would know that pestering knock anywhere. He wanted to disappear deeper into the water—but the water barely covered his rump.

The door opened a crack.

"Mayor Quill, sir?" It was Humphrey Hedgehog.

"What do you want?" the mayor barked. "I'm in the bath."

"I figured as much, sir."

Humphrey Hedgehog was the mayor's assistant deputy. By

now he had entered the private,
members-only watering hole.
Nothing bugged the mayor more
than when Humphrey considered
himself an equal.

"I'm covering my eyes, sir. I
won't see a thing. I just wanted
to let you know there seems to
be a problem with the water. It is
missing, sir."

"You don't say?" responded
Mayor Quill.

"Yes, sir. Indeed. Someone must
have stolen it. And I have a list

of possible culprits that I would like you to review at your earliest convenience." Humphrey flipped through at least ten pages on his clipboard.

Out of the corner of his eye, the mayor caught a glimpse of the top of Humphrey's list.

possible culprits

1. The Super Happy Party Bears

2. Thirsty Birds

The mayor looked down at his shallow bathwater. Some chunks of doughnut floated by, and rainbow sprinkles bobbed on the surface.

Squirrelly Sam suddenly appeared, scrambling down from the branches above to hang his head upside down in the doorway,

completely ignoring the sign out
front.

"Excuse me, Mr. Mayor. I have a
mail delivery for you."

Mayor Quill stomped his foot.
He shook from head to toe. Just
before the mayor exploded,
Humphrey rolled into a defensive
ball. Being a hedgehog, he had
his own spiny exterior. It came in
handy at times like these.

41

Quills exploded
everywhere. One narrowly
missed Arlo's ear. Another speared
the mail, tearing it out
of Sam's paw and
pinning it to a
tree several
feet away.
Humphrey
peeked out
from behind his
clipboard.

"Good shot, sir."

42

CHAPTER FOUR

Mayor Quill never got his bath. Soon City Hall was crawling with complainers about the water situation. No, really. Folks *actually* climbed onto the rotten upturned log and demanded a town meeting.

As Mayor Quill prepared to

address his people, Humphrey made preparations of his own.

"Excuse me, Humphrey," said Sam as he skittered in circles around Humphrey's short legs. Nothing made Squirrelly Sam squirrellier than when he had a big juicy piece of gossip to share. "You didn't hear this from me, but . . ."

Humphrey didn't hear it at all. Nothing could distract the assistant deputy. He was busy practicing the speech he would give to the Super Happy Party Bears.

"It has come to City Hall's attention," muttered Humphrey, "that you have stolen our water. Your shenanigans have gone on far too long, and it is upon order of the mayor himself that I must ask you to relocate." Humphrey chuckled to himself. This was a moment he had dreamed of often. And this was a speech he had rehearsed every night in his dreams, too. Getting rid of the Super Happy Party Bears would

surely make him a hero in the
Grumpy Woods. And heroes can
become mayors.

By now Sam was on top of
Humphrey's head, struggling to
make eye contact upside down.

" . . . gnashing and gnawing with
their ginormous teeth. Are you
listening, Humphrey?"

It was evident by
Humphrey's
glazed-over
eyes that he was
not listening to
Sam's story but
was instead daydreaming of his
mayoral inauguration party.

Sam sighed exasperatedly and
began all over again.

Humphrey fought to half listen,
catching bits and pieces—
"... newcomers ... all night long ...
TIIIIIMBERRRRR!"—until Mayor

Quill took the podium, signaling
the beginning of the town meeting.

But before the mayor even
finished clearing his throat, a
voice rang out from the crowd.
"My beautiful Grumpy River.
Someone stole it! Now I will never
finish my book!" cried out Bernice
Bunny.

Bernice was known to sit for hours on the banks of the Grumpy River with her twitchy nose stuck in a book.

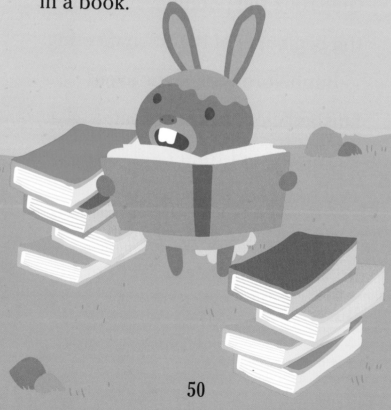

Everyone in Grumpy Woods knew to tiptoe by quietly. Bernice hated to be interrupted. Rumor had it that she'd been reading the same book for five years because the Super Happy Party Bears disturbed her so many times she had to keep reading the same paragraph over and over and over.

Frantic murmurs bubbled up from the gathered bunch.

"Stolen?"

"Gone?"

"The *whole* river?"

"Makes sense," said Mayor
Quill. "I once heard the Super
Happy Party Bears planning a pool
party. But they don't have a pool!"

The group gasped.

Humphrey worked out his own
prediction. "I know they were
making doughnuts this morning.

Large quantities of sugary
doughnuts can make one awfully
thirsty. All they would need is a
giant straw and *slurp!* The water
would be all sucked up."

"Well, you didn't hear it from
me, but—" started Squirrelly
Sam. And he was right. No one
heard him. They were all too busy

talking over one another, accusing
the Super Happy Party Bears of
ruining the river.

"Please! Everybody! One at a
time," yelled Mayor Quill as he
banged his gavel on the podium.

"All night I tossed and turned
to the terrible sound of crunching
and chewing!"

"There are mountains of
sawdust where trees once stood!"

"Dirty, dirty, dirty. Too much to clean," sang Dawn Fawn, who sang whenever she felt nervous. She really liked to keep things clean. Sometimes she even used Bernice's tail as a dust mop.

"Obviously, they are making lounge chairs for their pool party," stated Bernice matter-of-factly as she slowly stepped away from Dawn.

"Or they are making Popsicles

again," said Humphrey, "and need more sticks."

Sam excitedly continued his previous tale. By now he was so out of breath he was only speaking in fragments. "It's the monsters. Draining water. Obliterating trees. All night long. TIIIIIMMMBBBEEEERRRRR!"

"There are no monsters in the Grumpy Woods," interrupted Mayor Quill, who was finally listening to Sam.

"I wouldn't be too ssssure of that," came a hiss from the ground. It was Sherry Snake, self-proclaimed sheriff of the Grumpy Woods. Sherry made it her duty

57

to secure and protect the borders of the Grumpy Woods. Mostly, she just enjoyed telling other animals to scram.

"M-m-m-monsters?" Bernice's fuzzy ears trembled.

"Really, Sherry, this isn't helping," harrumphed Humphrey.

"I told them to sssstay out," continued Sherry, "but they ssssaid ssssnakessssskin was so lasssst sssspring and laughed at me."

"This doesn't make sense," said Mayor Quill.

"Exactly. Ssssnakessssskin is alwayssss in sssseasssson."

"I'll tell you what doesn't make sense," echoed a voice from the back. It was Opal Owl, pulling a curler out of her feathers and plucking bits of her nest from her waist. "It is morning and I am awake! I thought we all gave a hoot about peace and quiet."

"Our deepest apologies, Opal," said Mayor Quill. But before he could promise to keep the noise level down, the ground rumbled. The leaves rustled.

"It can't be," mumbled the mayor.

The Grumpy Woods neighbors' greatest fear was rolling by City Hall.

The welcome wagon.

Covered with welcome banners,
signs, and pennants, it was packed
with everything a good neighbor
needs to greet newcomers:
casseroles, cups of sugar to
borrow, fruit baskets, and muffins.

There was even a red carpet tied to the front, ready to be rolled out.

The wagon was being pulled along by the Super Happy Party Bears.

"There will be no welcoming in the Woods as stated by Mayoral Decree one-point-three-A!" Humphrey called after the wagon.

"Sssstop them!" hissed Sherry.

And all the townscritters
got in line after the bears
and headed down to the river.
When the Super Happy Party
Bears realized they were being
followed, they cheered.
"WE LOVE PARADES!" they
shouted, and marched that
sourpuss of a procession straight
to the monsters.

CHAPTER FIVE

There on the banks of the Grumpy
River was not a pair of monsters
but a pair of beavers. Next to the
pair of beavers was a heap of
sticks, logs, trunks, and twigs of
all shapes and sizes. The wood
was twisted and woven together

to create a mound that stretched
across the river and held back the
flow of water. Upriver the water
bulged and swelled. Yet downriver
it was barely a trickle.

The beavers hoisted more trees,
one by one, onto the pile.

"Truly magnificent," said one
beaver.

"Absolutely. The best river views in all of real estate," replied the other beaver.

"Nothing but the best for my Mitzi-witzy," responded the first beaver.

The Grumpy Woods residents stayed back, their mouths hanging open. But then the Super Happy Party Bears sprang into action.

"WELCOME TO THE GRUMPY WOODS!" they cheered, and rolled out the red carpet—literally.

"Oh dear," said the beaver named Mitzi, obviously startled. "Nelson, I thought you said this was a *secluded* area."

"Why, yes, Mitzi darling. Apparently these *bears* are a bit lost." And then under his breath to the bears, Nelson said, "Get lost."

"We're not lost," said Mops. "We're your neighbors!"

At the word *neighbors*, Mitzi practically fainted.

Three more beavers suddenly

poked their heads out from the pile of trees and leaves in the middle of the river. "What's all the commotion?" they asked. "It woke the baby."

"Oh, nothing, Devon. Nothing to worry about, Cricket. Just some riffraff passing by."

"We brought a casserole," said the littlest bear.

Nelson approached, sniffed the casserole, and then passed it off to Devon. "This might work to seal up that crack in the foundation."

Meanwhile, Cricket and Mitzi inspected the red carpet for possible use in their beaver lodge perched on top of the dam.

"Very well," said Nelson. "Now, if you don't mind, we are on a bit of a schedule."

"But we haven't played our icebreaker name game yet," said Jacks. "You go first, Nelson, so we can learn your name."

"My name is Nelson."

"No. Say something like, 'My name is Nelson, and I'm bringing noodles to the party.'"

"I am *not* bringing any noodles."

"Nuts?"

"No."

"Napkins?"

"Nope."

"You have to bring something, Nelson," explained Shades. "So that we learn your name."

"My name is Nelson, and apparently I'm bringing nincompoops to the party."

"HELLO, NELSON!" cheered the bears.

"HUG TIME!"

Nelson, however, was saved as Mayor Quill stepped forward.

"Allow me to introduce *my*self," he said. "I am Quill, mayor of the Grumpy Woods."

The littlest bear pouted. "Quilly, you aren't playing correctly! You always say, 'My name is Mayor

Quill, and I am bringing *quiet* to the party.' Silly Quilly!"

"Listen, I do appreciate this little shindig or whatever," said Nelson, "but I really must be getting back to work. Dams don't build themselves, you know."

"Can we have a tour when it's finished?" asked Mops.

"Certainly," said Nelson
sarcastically. "I can think of
nothing more thrilling. In fact, let's
sell tickets."

Mayor Quill chuckled. "Hee-hee.
Silly bears." He winked at Nelson
to prove he understood how
annoying the bears were.
"No one is taking
any tours. Now, if
we could all
just give the
beavers

some space, they can pack up and move on."

Nelson chuckled. "Hee-hee. Silly mayor. No one is packing up and moving on. Now, if you all could kindly get off my property . . ."

"*Your* property?" fumed Mayor Quill. "This is the Grumpy Woods!"

"Ah yes. And so I say, quite *grumpily*, YOU ARE NOT WELCOME HERE!" announced Nelson. And he waddled off, using his big flat tail to slam the door of the lodge behind him.

CHAPTER SIX

Between the quill storms and the many decrees he had written, the mayor was going to be bald by dinnertime.

"'Mayoral Decree two hundred thirty-eight,'" Mayor Quill read aloud as he wrote. "'Beavers are a nuisance and should be treated as such.'"

"Well said, sir," said Humphrey. "How dare they speak to you like that!"

"Ssssomething sssshould be done," said Sherry.

"We should write them a letter," suggested Bernice Bunny.

"No more mail," groaned
Mayor Quill, still reeling from his
morning visit to the Party Patch.
He continued writing. "'Mayoral
Decree two hundred thirty-nine:
The welcome wagon shall be rolled
off Grumpy Cliff immediately.'"

"Whoooomever heard of a
welcome wagon?" scoffed Opal.

80

"We will *un*welcome that wagon. *Smash! Crash!*" added Bernice.

"I can think of a few other things I'd like to roll off Grumpy Cliff," mumbled Humphrey.

"That's it!" said Mayor Quill. "Let's *un*welcome the beavers!"

"You want to roll them off the cliff?" asked Dawn.

"No, no," answered Quill. "I suggest we make an *un*welcome sign."

Humphrey waggled his spines. "Most excellent, sir. Once the beavers realize they are unwelcome, they will surely move on!"

Everyone grumbled about it, but no one had a better idea, so they got to work.

Sam's bushy tail made the perfect scary brushstrokes when dipped in berry juice. Dawn Fawn provided a pile of burrs collected during her most recent sweeping of the Woods. And when Sheriff Sherry set her mind to it, her fangs did some amazing whittling.

When they were done, the sign was drippy. It was spiky. And it was *un*welcoming.

To show their solidarity, the townscritters took the sign to the river shore by the beavers' dam. Together, they smacked it into the ground.

As they proudly marched away,

Mayor Quill glanced back and
was sure he could see four pairs
of beady eyes peering out from
the lodge. He was certain it would
be only a matter of time until the
beavers packed their things and
left to clog up someone else's river
someplace far away.

And maybe that would have
happened . . . if the Super Happy

Party Bears hadn't gone to the riverbank, too, just after them.

"What a beautiful sign," they squealed. After all, it was prickly and reminded them of their beloved mayor. "What a wonderful idea!"

"'Unwelcome to the Grumpy Woods,'" read Mops. "What do you suppose that means?"

"It's actually 'UN Welcome to the Grumpy Woods,'" explained

Bubbles, briefly pausing his bubble blowing. "There's a space. It stands for *United Neighbors Welcome to the Grumpy Woods*."

"YAY! We LOVE the United Neighbors!" cheered the bears. "We should go to their next meeting."

"And bring doughnuts," added the littlest bear.

"Kindly get off our lawn!" came a voice from inside the lodge.

"NELSON!" cheered the bears.

"We came to retrieve our casserole dish," said Shades. "No worries if you didn't have time to wash it and fill it up with something equally tasty. We understand that moving can be stressful."

"What's that sign?" asked Nelson.

"On behalf of the United Neighbors," proclaimed Mops, "we

welcome you, once again, to the
Grumpy Woods."

The bears did a dance.

Slide to the right.

Hop to the left.

Shimmy, shimmy, shake.

Strike a pose.

CHAPTER SEVEN

The four beavers came outside
and stood gazing up at the ghastly
sign. The baby beaver cried.

"It's quite tacky, isn't it?"
whispered Devon.

"Truly," agreed Mitzi as quietly
as her rising blood pressure would

allow. "Next thing you know, these bears will be bringing us a pink plastic flamingo."

"Isn't it beautiful?" gushed the bears.

"Not quite the word I would choose," muttered Cricket.

"It makes mine look so teeny," said the littlest bear. He held up

a sign with a bow around its post

and a tag that read:

To: my favoritest neighbors

From: littlest bear

Painted on the sign were a

garden gnome and the words

gnome
Sweet
gnome

"Oh, puns. How quaint," said

Mitzi, rolling her eyes.

"Puns are a sign of language mastery," stated Bubs.

"But the United Neighbors sign is so much more beautiful," said littlest bear, holding back tears.

Just then Nelson had an idea.

"Well, it seems to me that *United Neighbors* means that this sign could be placed *anywhere* in the woods. It's for *all* of us. While the gnome sign is a very special gift."

Cricket caught on quickly. "Oh yes. This humongous sign belongs where *others* can enjoy it."

"It would be a *crime* to keep it to ourselves," added Devon.

"We LOVE sharing!" cheered the bears. "Just wait until Quilly sees

this beautiful sign in front of City
Hall, where everyone can enjoy it!"

And that was that. The sign
went to City Hall. And the beavers
stayed.

As for the GNOME, SWEET GNOME
sign? Well, let's just say that the
beavers got a new doormat.

"Unwelcoming *us*?" said Mayor

Quill when he found the sign the next day. "The nerve of those beavers!"

"If they won't leave," said Humphrey, "then we will have to find a way to keep them out. Here's my new idea to unwelcome them: We will build a wall." He unrolled blueprints for a giant wall along the riverbank. "Sherry can patrol from the ground. Sam will be able to spy from the tree branches above," he explained.

Everyone liked the idea. But no one cheered. They were too grumpy for that.

Instead, they got to work constructing the tallest, most towering wall ever.

Sam and Bernice were on saw— or gnaw—duty.

Opal flew high to hold the logs in place as Humphrey hammered

them together using quills. (Don't
ask where he got those from.)

Mayor Quill shouted orders. No
surprise there.

And Dawn, of course, was
on cleanup duty.

It was quite a team effort.
The wall was twenty-
four Sherrys long and eight
Sherrys tall. Sherry had
objected to being used as
a ruler, but since they had
no proper measuring
instruments, she was
forced to cooperate.
When the wall

was finished, the townscritters weren't the only ones applauding.

"A gated community! How wonderful," gushed Mitzi, a tear in her eye.

"Absolutely dreamy!" exclaimed Cricket.

Devon chuckled. "Seems we've seen the last of the riffraff."

"Good riddance," said Nelson.

But they had spoken too soon.

"A howdy and a half, neighbors!"

It was the bears. Apparently,

twenty-four Sherrys long was not

long enough. The bears simply

walked around the wall.

"My, what persistent little legs

you have, to go so long out of your

way to see us," said Mitzi, smiling

with clenched teeth.

"A wall between neighbors is

never long," stated Bubbles, who

then blew a huge, shiny bubble

that popped right on Nelson's

nose. POP!

The Super Happy Party

Bears loved visiting their new

neighbors—which really meant standing near the beavers, oohing and aahing over everything the beavers said, and occasionally breaking into a dance. The beavers had long ago decided that the only way to handle this kind of visit was to "not look them in the eye and hope they go away." So far it hadn't worked.

Over tea, the beavers were discussing the almost-finished lodge made of logs and leaves and sticks. They ignored the bears.

"Oh, how I wish we could create that sunroom," Mitzi said with a sigh. "It would be the absolute perfect spot where you could work on the Sunday crossword puzzle, Nelson."

"Indeed," agreed Cricket. "And imagine the stargazing we could do at night, Devon."

Although Devon and Nelson wished to add a sunroom to the lodge, there was one very big issue.

"Unfortunately," said Nelson, "we are running out of logs."

"It's a pity there just isn't enough lumber." Devon sighed.

At that, the Super Happy Party Bears, excited to be of help, chimed in. "We know where there is plenty more wood!"

You see, there was a big flaw in the townscritters' plan. The only building material available in the Grumpy Woods was . . . well, wood.

And beavers chew wood and use it to build things. You can imagine what happened to the massive wooden fence—go ahead and imagine it.

There was a lot of chewing and gnawing, and by the next morning, Nelson, Devon, Mitzi, and Cricket had the sunroom they'd always wanted.

CHAPTER EIGHT

The Grumpy Woods was becoming the Even Grumpier Woods.

The unwelcome sign had disappeared. The gigantic fence had disappeared. The beavers had *not* disappeared, and they didn't seem to have any plans to do so.

Instead, the dam and the lodge
on top got bigger—just like the
townscritters' tempers.

"We need to come up with
another plan, sir," said Humphrey.

"Do you think I don't know
that?" Mayor Quill snapped.
Humphrey noticed the mayor's
quills beginning to tremble and
feared another quill storm.

"Whoever thought that ssssilly wall would work, anyhow?" complained Sherry.

"Who are you calling s-s-s-s-silly?" snapped Humphrey.

"Could you-hooooo keep it down? Some of us were ruuuudely awoken," hooted Opal.

"You didn't hear this from me, but . . ." started Sam.

111

"NOT NOW!" everyone shouted.

"It's hopeless! I NEED MY DUST BUNNY!" sang Dawn. The destruction of the wall had left behind piles of sawdust that Dawn was frantically trying to sweep up.

"Ack! No you don't!" protested Bernice. Bernice hated being used as Dawn's duster even more than she hated being interrupted while reading.

"MUST CLEAN!

MUST DUST, MUST DUST, MUST

DUST!" Dawn sang out.

"QUIET!" yelled Mayor Quill.

"The last thing anyone wants to

hear right now is your singing.

If you don't stop, *I'm* going to leave the Grumpy Woods!"

"Sir, that's it, sir!" said Humphrey, perking up. "I have a plan! What's worse than Dawn's singing?"

No one had an answer.

"You, sir. *You* singing!"

"I beg your pardon," said Mayor Quill.

"Not *just* you, sir. All of us."

"Speak for yourself," hooted
Opal.

"All right, maybe not Opal. But
no one ever said, *Just listen to the
beautiful sounds of that porcupine.*
Or *hedgehog*! Or *squirrel*! If we
become the Grumpy Woods
Chorus, we can serenade those

lumberjacks until they can't take it anymore!"

"My aunt Marty always did complain about my singing," admitted Sam.

"Rabbits are known to be unable to carry a tune. I read that in a book," said Bernice.

So off the townscritters went, looking like holiday carolers with attitude.

When they got to the lodge, they found the bears already

there, throwing a housewarming

party for their new neighbors.

"Look!" said the littlest bear.

"Everyone else came to the party,

too!" He clapped his paws in delight.

"SUPER HAPPY NEW HOME!" cheered the bears. "Let the housewarming party begin!"

"Hand out the doughnuts," added Mops.

Slide to the right.

Hop to the left.

Shimmy, shimmy, shake.

Strike a pose.

The sun was starting to set, and the beavers were indeed celebrating the completion of their new home . . . while doing their best to ignore the other animals around them.

"Simply lovely," said Nelson.

"Oh yes, lovely," agreed Mitzi.

"To fabulous new views and horizons," declared Devon.

"Most definitely," added Cricket.

The bears applauded in the background. "This is the most special day ever!"

"I actually have gifts for all of us," announced Mitzi, trying hard to ignore the bears and their party dance. *"Earmuffs!"* Mitzi pulled out five pairs of homemade earmuffs, perfectly sized for four adult beavers and one baby beaver who wanted to pretend that a group of Super Happy Party Bears was not dancing around them.

"Huzzah!" cheered the beavers, and they clinked their glasses.

At that moment, a sound rose

up from the riverbank as the townscritters decided to add their own bit of flavor to the party. It was an ear-splitting combination of howling, yowling, and weepy screeching.

The townscritters gave it their all. But the beavers, under their earmuffs, didn't hear a thing.

CHAPTER NINE

The sun went down and the stars came out. The townscritters kept singing louder and louder and louder, but it didn't do any good. The beavers just relaxed in their sunroom, enjoying the views that only the best real estate along the Grumpy River could provide.

Meanwhile, the bears cheered and chatted and cheered some more, never even caring that their new neighbors simply smiled politely and nodded gently so as to not disrupt the earmuffs atop their heads.

At one point, Mitzi drew the curtains, hoping not to even have to *look* at the bears partying on her lawn. But the bears simply exclaimed, "We LOVE shadow puppet shows!" and continued to party.

Gasping for breath and turning blue, the townscritters felt like failures once again.

"Maybe if Mayor Quill sings a solo . . ." suggested Sam.

The mayor's quills began to quake. A storm was brewing.

"No one needs to sing a solo, sir," Humphrey assured him. "I think if we sing for one more hour . . ." But glares from the other townscritters stopped Humphrey's thought.

"That's it!" fumed the mayor. "I'm putting an end to this. I will demand that they leave. After all, I am the MAYOR! It will be decreed!"

And he marched right up to the door of the lodge, but before he could knock—

"QUILLY!" cheered the bears. "You've come to the celebration!"

"This is no time to celebrate," said the mayor.

"Quilly, come dance with us!" begged the bears. They dragged Mayor Quill onto the dam and stuck a cup of juice in his hand. "SHIMMY, SHIMMY, SHAKE!" they chanted.

The dam shook. In fact, it shook the earmuffs right off of Nelson's head.

"This is an outrage!" said Nelson, poking his head out of the lodge. "Stop that this instant!"

But the bears continued to party.

Seeing how much the beavers were bothered by the dancing, the townscritters suddenly developed an interest in dancing, too.

"Oh, sir, those are some mighty fine dance moves," said Humphrey, joining in.

"I feel the beat in my feet!" said Bernice as she stomped and kicked her back feet. "Come on, Dawn, let's clean up this dance floor!"

In spite of themselves, the residents of the Grumpy Woods got their groove on.

The dam trembled. The logs quivered. The carefully constructed lodge started to creak.

"Nelson, do something!" shrieked Mitzi.

"I'm getting seasick," moaned Devon.

"It's a housewarming party!" cheered the bears. "Welcome home!"

Slide to the right.

Hop to the left.

Shimmy,
shimmy, shake.

Strike a pose.

By now the dam was really
hopping. Mayor Quill almost lost
his balance, and grabbed on to
Mops's tail for balance.

"CONGA LINE!" cheered Mops.

The conga line quickly formed
and made its way toward the shore,
with all the critters in tow. The

littlest bear brought up the rear, and as he jumped from the beaver dam to shore, his wee paw pushed off *just* enough to finally dislodge the whole wooden structure.

With a great shudder, the logs splintered and gave way. The dam broke as the Grumpy River came roaring through with a giant *whoosh*, and the lodge washed away with the current.

Nelson, Mitzi, Devon, Cricket, and the baby scrambled to the roof.

"If I'd wanted a yacht,
I would have asked for a
yacht!" screamed Mitzi.

Cricket pouted. "Next time we're
hiring contractors."

Nelson and Devon put on their
earmuffs. It was going to be a long
ride downstream.

Back on shore, the bears waved
good-bye to the beavers. "How
clever of them to turn their house
into a houseboat," said Shades.

"When living on a houseboat,"
stated Bubs, "the world is your
backyard."

"BON VOYAGE! HAVE A GREAT CRUISE!" cheered the bears as they continued waving from the bank of the river. And you know what?

The townscritters cheered, too.

They were feeling just a *little* less grumpy. THE END.

ABOUT THE AUTHOR

In previous chapters, Marcie Colleen has been a teacher, an actress, and a nanny, but now she gets to write children's books while eating triple-decker giggle-and-jelly sandwiches in her pajamas! She lives with her husband and their mischievous sock monkey in San Diego, California, where every day is the best day ever. This is her debut chapter book.

Don't Miss the other
SUPER HAPPY PARTY BEARS
BOOK